Mrs. Claus

TAKES A

VACATION

Linas Alsenas

SCHOLASTIC INC.

New York Toronto London Auckland Sydney
Mexico City New Delhi Hong Kong Buenos Aires

Mrs. Claus had never taken a vacation in her life.

This year, she was determined to go traveling.

"Snow, snow, and more snow!" she told Santa. "Well, I'm
tired of it! You get to see the whole world every year.
Now it's my turn. Let's see how *you* like sitting at home!"

She packed her bags, hitched a reindeer to the sleigh,
and waved good-bye to Santa.

"Don't worry, dear. I'll be home before Christmas Eve!"

But with each passing day, Santa *did* worry.

"Mrs. Claus isn't used to warm weather," thought Santa.
"She'll get sunburned!"

But Mrs. Claus didn't mind the sun at all.

"She doesn't know all the world's languages,"
thought Santa, "and she has never been around
so many different kinds of people."

"I'll bet she's terribly lonely!"

But Mrs. Claus had no trouble making friends.

"She must miss gingerbread cookies," thought Santa...

...as he baked his first batch ever.

But Mrs. Claus didn't miss
gingerbread cookies at all.
Well...maybe a little bit.

"And I'll bet she wishes she were here to help
with Christmas preparations," thought Santa...

...as he put up decorations around the house.

Mrs. Claus didn't give the house a passing thought. But she did wish Santa could have been with her.

"Mrs. Claus will be so disappointed to have missed decorating the tree," thought Santa as he hung the last ornament.

Mrs. Claus did miss decorating
the tree. She started seeing
Christmas trees everywhere.

And wreaths.

And snowmen.

And mistletoe.

She knew it was time
to go back home.

Mrs. Claus returned on Christmas Eve Day. Santa greeted her with a big hug and a kiss.

"Home at last!" he said.

After dinner, Mrs. Claus showed Santa souvenirs from her vacation.

Soon, Santa had to get ready for his trip.

He pulled on his boots, put on his mittens, and handed
Mrs. Claus her coat. "What's this?" she asked.

"I know you've probably had your fill of traveling,"
Santa said, "but how about one more ride with me?"